Open -
happy to see you!

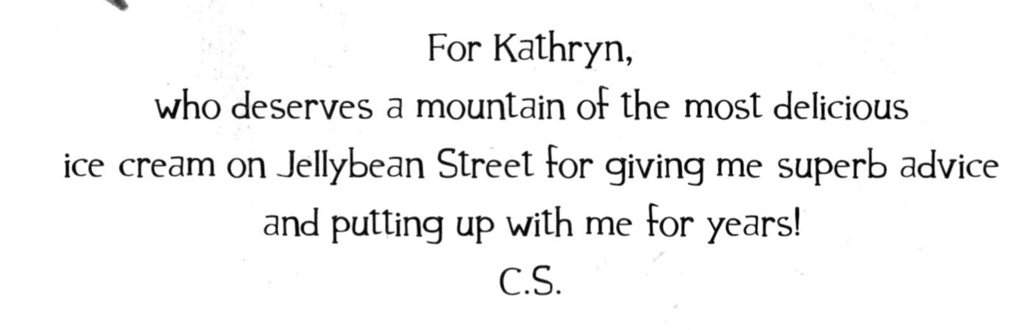

For Kathryn,
who deserves a mountain of the most delicious
ice cream on Jellybean Street for giving me superb advice
and putting up with me for years!
C.S.

For Onno, Penelope, and Ian,
whose favourite ice cream flavours are mango,
butter pecan, and dark chocolate.
N.O.

First published in 2016 by Scholastic Children's Books
Euston House, 24 Eversholt Street
London NW1 1DB
a division of Scholastic Ltd
www.scholastic.co.uk
London ~ New York ~ Toronto ~ Sydney ~ Auckland
Mexico City ~ New Delhi ~ Hong Kong

ISBN 978 1407 14810 6

Printed in China

1 3 5 7 9 10 8 6 4 2

Gorilla Loves Vanilla

Written by
Chae Strathie

Illustrated by
Nicola O'Byrne

SCHOLASTIC

If you take a walk down **Jellybean Street,**
There's a wonderful place you can go for a treat.

A **fabulous** store full of **yummy** ice cream –
The kind of ice cream that makes everyone beam!

Little Sam Sundae is known as the king
Of cornets and wafers and flavours that ZING!

And one sunny day
as Sam opened the store,
Five hungry animals
dashed through the door.

First in the line was a mouse
who squeaked,
"Please,
May I have a sundae
that tastes of blue cheese."

Now that might sound **scrumptious**
to little grey mice,
But none of the others thought
cheese ice was nice.

It sounded quite **stinky**, but Sam didn't blink –
He rustled up cheesy ice cream in a wink.

Next to step up was a stripy ship's cat
With whiskery cheeks and a white sailor's hat.

"My favourite," he said, "is a sailing cat's wish.
Bring me fish finger ice cream in a dish!"

It sounded quite **yucky**,
but Sam didn't blink –
He rustled up fishy ice cream
in a wink.

The chicken said,
"I'll have a cone full of **worms** –
I like nothing more
than an ice cream that squirms."

"It's funny the way that it wriggles and jiggles,
It tickles my beak and it gives me the giggles!"

It sounded
too **squirmy**,
but Sam didn't blink –
He rustled up **wormy ice cream** in a wink.

The flavour the cow chose was **daisies** and **grass**
Sprinkled with dandelions in a tall glass.
"It's simply a-moo-zing!"
she gleefully cheered.
But all of her friends thought
her flavour was weird.
Sam

It sounded **revolting**,
but Sam didn't blink –
He rustled up
daisy ice cream in a wink.

The hippo stomped up with a thump and a thud,
And asked for a cone filled with
mountains of **mud**!

"I don't want to eat it," he said with a laugh.
"I'm going to jump in

It sounded quite **messy**, but Sam didn't blink –
He rustled up muddy ice cream in a wink.

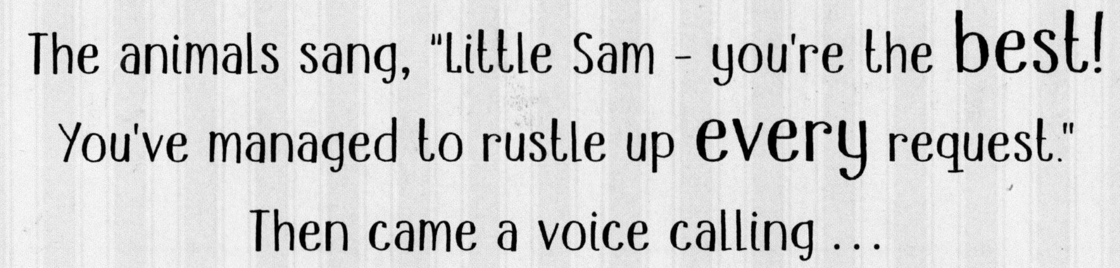

The animals sang, "Little Sam – you're the **best!**
You've managed to rustle up **every** request."
Then came a voice calling …

"I want some too."

A gorilla
was there at the
end of the queue!

"I don't want **fish fingers**
or **worms** from the chiller,
Just give me a cone full of . . .
good **old vanilla.**"

The others agreed that
they'd all been too hasty –
None of their flavours
seemed **nearly** as tasty.

Sam served a cone that was everyone's dream -
Scoop upon **scoop** of amazing ice cream!

He topped it with
sprinkles

and **milk
chocolate**
chips.

The sticky
fudge sauce
made them all
lick their lips.

The animals gasped - they couldn't help staring,
And lucky for them . . .

Gorillas LOVE sharing!

Sam

Closed -
see you soon!